This edition published by Parragon Books Ltd in 2015

Parragon Books Ltd
Chartist House
15–17 Trim Street
Bath BA1 1HA, UK
www.parragon.com

ISBN 978-1-4748-1221-4

Printed in China

Bath • New York • Cologne • Melbourne • Delhi
Hong Kong • Shenzhen • Singapore • Amsterdam

"Hey, Woody! Ready to go to Cowboy Camp?" Andy cried, bursting into the bedroom.

Woody was very excited about camp, though he couldn't show his feelings to Andy. Toys were supposed to stay motionless whenever people could see them.

Andy grabbed Woody and Buzz for a quick adventure. Suddenly, there was a loud *RIIIPPPP!* Woody's shoulder had ripped open!

Sadly, Andy handed Woody to his mum, who placed
the cowboy doll up on the highest shelf in the room.
        Woody watched sadly as Andy left without him.
What if Andy never played with him again?
        And Woody didn't feel any better when he found Wheezy,
a toy penguin, who'd been sitting broken on the shelf
for months. Maybe that would be Woody's future, too....

Later that day, Andy's mum put on a garage sale. She came into Andy's room and chose Wheezy as one of the sale items!

Thinking quickly, Woody waited until Andy's mum was out of sight, then whistled for Andy's puppy. Together, they sneaked outside, grabbed Wheezy and headed back to safety. But because his arm was injured, Woody tumbled to the ground.

Then, a strange man noticed Woody, picked him up ...

... and stole him!

From their upstairs window, the other toys watched in horror as the man threw Woody into the boot of his car.

Buzz couldn't let Woody be taken away so easily, so he jumped out of the window and slid down the drainpipe.

But Buzz was too late – the car sped away.

The strange man took Woody to his apartment and locked him in. Woody looked around for a way to escape.

POP! A packing box suddenly burst open and Woody was knocked off his feet by a galloping toy horse.

"Yee-haw! It's really you!" shouted a cowgirl.

The cowgirl said she was Jessie and the horse was Bullseye. Then she introduced the Prospector, a toy who had never been out of his box. All of them were thrilled to see Woody!

Jessie turned on the television and a programme called *Woody's Roundup!* came on. It starred Jessie, Stinky Pete the Prospector, Bullseye and ... Sheriff Woody!

Woody couldn't believe it. He had once been a television star! The Prospector explained that the *Roundup* toys had become valuable collectibles. The man who had taken Woody planned to sell them all, as a set, to a Japanese museum!

Meanwhile, Buzz and the other toys had worked out that it was Al, the owner of Al's Toy Barn, that had taken Woody. They set out to rescue their friend.

Together, with a little help from Slinky, they jumped off the roof.

"To Al's Toy Barn ... and beyond!" Buzz cried.

After a long walk, the toys finally reached Al's Toy Barn. They just needed to cross one last, very busy, street.

Luckily, Buzz noticed a pile of orange traffic cones. He told everyone to grab one and then, slowly, they ventured across the street, hiding under the cones. Soon, the street was filled with skidding, honking, crashing cars, all trying to avoid the strange, moving traffic cones!

But the toys barely noticed. They had arrived at Al's Toy Barn.

Inside Al's Toy Barn, aisles of shiny new toys
seemed to stretch into the distance. Everyone looked
up in awe – how would they ever find Woody in here?

Back at Al's apartment, an old man had arrived
to give Woody a makeover. The man opened a wooden
case with special trays and drawers full of toy parts
and doll paint. He cleaned Woody's eyes and ears, and
repainted the top of the cowboy's head, where the paint
had worn away. He even polished Woody's boots.

Best of all, he sewed up the rip in Woody's arm!

Once the toy cleaner had left, Woody told Jessie that he couldn't go to the museum, because he had to get back to Andy.

Jessie sadly explained that she had once had an owner – a wonderful little girl called Emily. But when Emily grew up, she abandoned Jessie.

"You never forget kids like Emily or Andy," said Jessie. "But they forget you."

Woody began to worry that Andy would forget about him one day, too.

Back in Al's Toy Barn, Buzz found an aisle full of brand-new, updated Buzz Lightyear toys! He reached out to touch one of the fancy new utility belts and suddenly a hand clamped on to his wrist. It was a new Buzz Lightyear, who believed he'd caught a rogue space ranger!

New Buzz tied Old Buzz into a box and ran to join Andy's toys – and not one of them realized they'd left the real Buzz behind!

Outside, New Buzz was excited about his new mission! He quickly led everyone into Al's apartment building through an air vent.

"No time to lose!" he shouted.

Then, because he thought he was a real space ranger, he tried to fly up to the top floor! Luckily, the lift came by just in time and carried everyone up instead.

Sneaking through the air vents, the toys finally reached
Al's apartment. New Buzz rushed up to Bullseye and yelled,
"We're here, Woody!"

Andy's toys looked at the New Buzz suspiciously.
Then Andy's real Buzz appeared, having escaped the toy shelf
and caught up with the others. The toys were confused!

Finally, everyone worked out who was who. But that still
left one problem. "Woody," said the real Buzz. "We need
to leave now."

But Woody didn't want to leave. The *Roundup* gang needed him to make a complete set for the museum. Besides, what if Andy didn't want Woody anymore?

"You're a toy!" Buzz said. "Life's only worth living if you're being loved by a kid."

"This is my only chance," Woody protested.

Sadly, Buzz led Andy's toys towards home.

Soon, though, Woody realized that Buzz was right – he did
belong with Andy! He ran to the vent and called for his friends
to return. Then he turned to the *Roundup* gang. "Come with me,"
he said. "Andy will play with all of us, I know it!"

Jessie and Bullseye were excited ... but the Prospector blocked
their path! After a lifetime in his box, he was determined to go
to the museum.

Suddenly, Al returned! He packed the *Roundup* toys into a case
and headed out of the door.

Luckily, Buzz and the gang spotted Al leaving the building. They knew that Woody was inside his case and they had to help!

They jumped into a nearby pizza truck and, with Buzz at the steering wheel, Slinky on the pedals, Rex as navigator and Hamm working the gears, they followed Al's car all the way to the airport.

The toys couldn't walk openly through the airport, but luckily Buzz spotted a pet carrier. They piled inside, sticking their legs through the bottom so they could walk. Moving as quickly as they dared, the group followed Al and his green case.

Still in the pet carrier, Andy's toys climbed on to the luggage conveyer belt. Buzz finally found Al's case, but when he opened it – *POW!* – the Prospector jumped out and punched Buzz.

"Hey! No one does that to my friend," Woody yelled, tackling the Prospector.

With his pickaxe, the Prospector ripped open Woody's shoulder again. He was about to drag Woody back into the case, but Andy's toys arrived just in time to save him.

Bullseye kicked free from Al's case as the conveyor belt carried them outside, but Jessie was still stuck!

"Ride like the wind, Bullseye!" Woody yelled as he and Buzz jumped on Bullseye's back. They raced after the baggage truck. Woody finally scrambled onto the truck, but by then, the green case was already being loaded into a plane. Woody hid inside another suitcase and was tossed on to the plane, too.

Woody quickly found the scared cowgirl.

"C'mon, Jess," he said. "It's time to take you home."

But just then, the plane's doors closed. They were stuck inside!

Desperate, they crawled through a hatch, down to the plane's wheels. The plane was already speeding down the runway. Then Woody slipped! Jessie caught him just in time, but his arm was starting to rip even more.

Twirling his pull string, Woody tried a daring trick. First he lassoed a bolt on the wheels. Then he grabbed Jessie's hand and ...

... together, they swung towards the ground!

As the two hurtled down and under the plane, Woody's pull string unhooked from the bolt on the plane – throwing them right to Buzz, who was galloping along on Bullseye! Everyone was safe.

Watching the plane take off into the sky, Woody, Jessie, Buzz and Bullseye danced and cheered.

"That was definitely Woody's finest hour!" cried Jessie.

When Andy arrived home from Cowboy Camp,
he was surprised by what he found. "New toys!" he cried.
"Thanks, Mum!"

Jessie and Bullseye had joined all his favourites,
welcoming him home. Andy couldn't wait to play with
everyone ... right after he sewed up Woody's shoulder!

Someday Andy would grow up and maybe he would
stop playing with toys, but Woody and Buzz knew there
was no place they'd rather be. Besides, they'd always have
each other – for infinity and beyond!